ART DOG

by THACHER HURD

FOR STARR LATRONICA

HarperCollinsPublishers

Art Dog Copyright © 1996 by Thacher Hurd. Manufactured in China. All rights reserved.
Library of Congress Cataloging-in-Publication Data. Hurd, Thacher. Art dog / [written and illustrated] by Thacher Hurd.   p.   cm.
Summary: When the Mona Woofa is stolen from the Dogopolis Museum of Art, a mysterious character who calls himself Art Dog tracks down and
captures the thieves. ISBN 0-06-024424-0. — ISBN 0-06-024425-9 (lib. bdg.). — ISBN 0-06-443489-3 (pbk.) [1. Dogs—Fiction. 2. Artists—Fiction.] I. Title.
PZ7.H9562Ar 1996 95-31092 [E]—dc20 CIP AC Typography by Tom Starace ❖ Visit us on the World Wide Web! http://www.harperchildrens.com

Arthur Dog was a guard at the Dogopolis Museum of Art.
He liked his job.

He liked guarding the paintings by Vincent Van Dog and Pablo Poodle, but Leonardo Dog Vinci was Arthur's favorite painter— or was it Henri Muttisse? Arthur couldn't decide.

At night Arthur came home to his little apartment on West 17th Street,
made himself dinner, and read until it was time for bed.
Arthur led a quiet life. He seldom went out—
except on nights when the moon was full.

On those nights Arthur's eyes grew bright
and his fur seemed to glisten.
He would take out a box he kept in his closet,

put on a hat and a mask,
and tiptoe down the back stairs
into the streets of Dogopolis.

He crept down an alley,
and when he was sure no one was around,

he unlocked the box and took out . . .

paints and brushes.

He painted a slash of lightni...
a splash of sunshine, and c... ... of
glowing lights in the night.

He painted monsters ten feet tall,
fish with tails the size of houses,
frogs ready to hop over skyscrapers.

When he was finished he crept home, a dog alone,
wondering if anyone ever noticed his paintings.

No one saw him paint, or sign his paintings with a splat of his tail
and the name "Art Dog." No one knew who Art Dog really was . . .

until one night at the museum.
CRASH! A window was broken. A door was busted.
BRRRINGGGG! The alarm went off,
and footsteps clattered down the alley behind the museum.

The police screeched to the scene of the crime.
The director of the museum was not far behind.
"Yikes! The Mona Woofa's gone!" cried the museum director.
"Look what they left instead of a Leonardo Dog Vinci!"

"Is this art? Looks like a Mona Lulu to me," said the chief of police.
"The paint's still wet . . ." said the museum director.

"Find me the culprit!" barked the chief of police.

They nabbed the first dog they found in the alley.
His eyes had a certain glow to them,
and his fur seemed to glisten in the moonlight.
He also had a paintbrush in his paw.
"Book him," said the chief of police.

They threw him in jail, but . . .

when no one was looking, he pulled out a brush
and a tube of paint and he painted a ladder.

He climbed up the ladder,

and where there were bars,

he painted a window . . .

and jumped out,

back onto the streets of Dogopolis.
Then he put his nose in the air.
What was he sniffing?

Suddenly he took out his brush and his paints.
Zip! Splash! Smoosh!
He painted himself a Brushmobile with his name on the side.

He whizzed over to the Acme Paint factory to fill up his tank.

Then off he roared into the night—
over highways and bridges, through the park and past the ballet,
leaving a trail of paint behind him as he went.

He slammed on the brakes in front of a deserted warehouse.
He sniffed. He tiptoed. He looked inside.

Three nasty-looking mutts were getting ready to ship something
to a distant port. He took a closer look. It was the Mona!
"Yikes!"

The mutts turned around.

"Hey, whadda *you* doin' here?" said the biggest mutt.

"Gosh . . . I . . . errr . . . must have made a wrong turn," said Art Dog.

"You can say that again," said the mutts.

It looked like big trouble for Art Dog.

There was only one thing left to do:

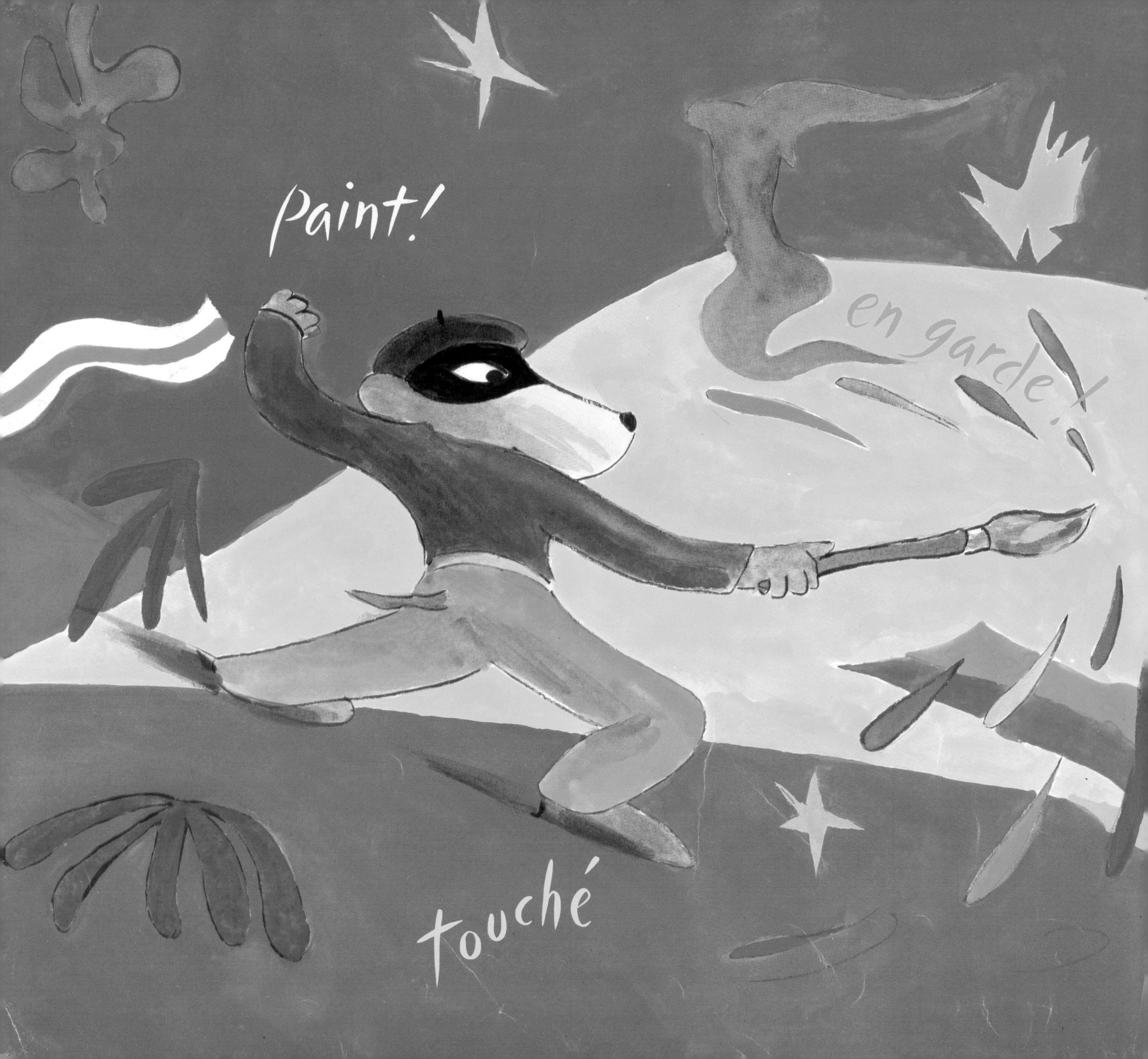
paint!
en garde!
touché

What a MESSTERPIECE!
"Wow!" said the chief of police, as he arrived with the museum director.
"How did you know where the Mona was?"
Art Dog wiggled his nose. "I can smell art a mile away."

The director of the museum said,
"I don't know how to thank you, Mr. . . ."
"Art Dog," said Art Dog, pointing to his Brushmobile.
"Art Dog, I like the way you paint. How about a show at the museum?"
"Sure thing," said Art Dog as he sped away in his Brushmobile.

Soon it was the night for Art Dog's show at the Dogopolis
Museum of Art.
Everyone stood around and sipped root beer as they waited
to meet Art Dog and see his paintings.

But where was he? Where were his paintings?
"And, for that matter," wondered the museum director,
"where's Arthur? He should be on the job tonight!"

Suddenly there was a sound.
Everyone rushed outside, just in time to see . . .

Art Dog, high in the sky,
finishing his masterpiece, *City Rhapsody*.
Everyone was amazed and speechless.

Then, suddenly, he was gone.
Who was Art Dog?
Who was this painter in a Brushmobile, catcher of crooks,
bringer of light to the Dogopolis night?

No one knew.